# MONTY + SYLVESTER

A TALE OF
EVERYDAY
ASTRONAUTS

BY CARLY GLEDHILL

FOR CATHERINE, CHARLOTTE, LAUREN, ROSIE AND SARAH – C.G.

ORCHARD BOOKS

First published in Great Britain in 2019
by The Watts Publishing Group

1 3 5 7 9 10 8 6 4 2

Text and illustrations © Carly Gledhill, 2019

A CIP catalogue record for this book is available
from the British Library.

HB ISBN: 978 1 40835 176 5
PB ISBN: 978 1 40835 177 2

Printed and bound in China

Orchard Books
An imprint of Hachette Children's Group
Part of The Watts Publishing Group Limited
Carmelite House 50 Victoria Embankment
London EC4Y 0DZ

An Hachette UK Company
www.hachette.co.uk

www.hachettechildrens.co.uk

# MONTY
# +
# SYLVESTER

## A TALE OF EVERYDAY ASTRONAUTS

ORCHARD

CARLY GLEDHILL

# MEET MONTY AND SYLVESTER.
# THEY'RE SPACE EXPLORERS (IN TRAINING).

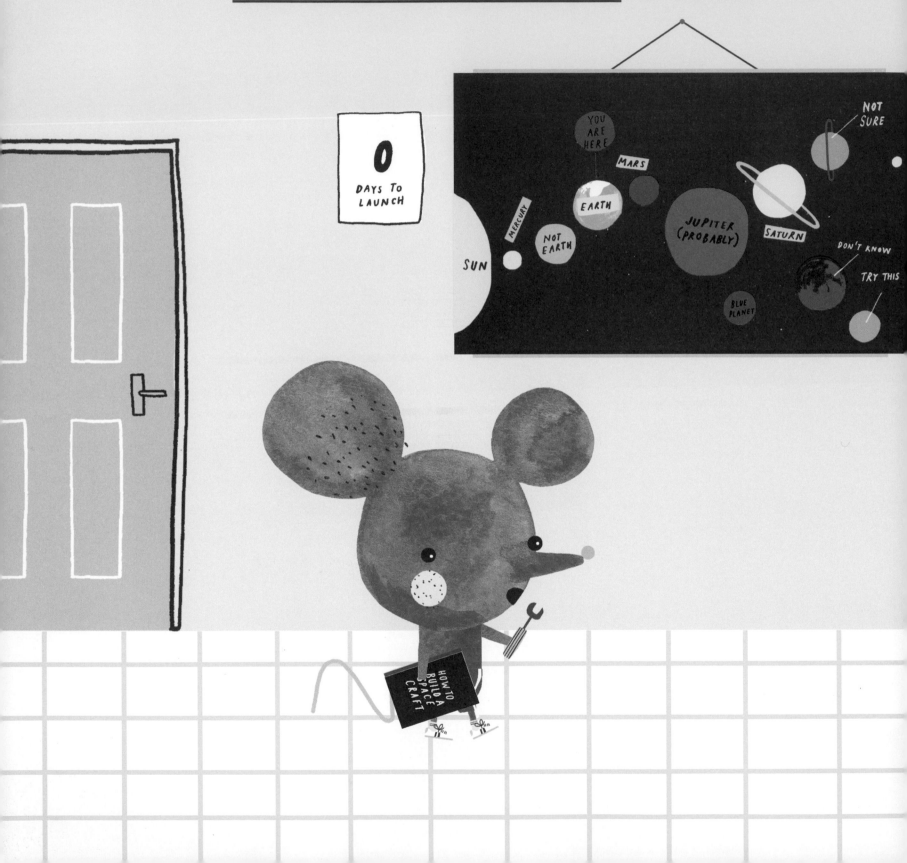

ASTRO LUNGE →

THEY HAVE BEEN TRAINING (FOR AT LEAST 20 MINUTES) FOR A SPECIAL MISSION:
TO TRAVEL TO DEEPEST, DARKEST SPACE, FIND AN UNDISCOVERED PLANET
AND BECOME FAMOUS ASTRONAUTS.

## FRIEND 1

YOU COULD GET CAUGHT IN A METEOR SHOWER

## FRIEND 2

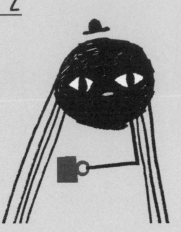

YOU KNOW THAT TUCKING YOUR TROUSERS INTO YOUR SOCKS DOESN'T MAKE THEM AIR-TIGHT, DON'T YOU?

## FRIEND 3

THERE AREN'T ANY UNDISCOVERED PLANETS LEFT

## FRIEND 4

YOU JUST WON'T MAKE IT!

* GULP *

IGNORING THEIR FRIENDS, MONTY AND SYLVESTER BRAVELY CLIMB THE LAST SMALL STEPS TO THE LAUNCH PAD.

# MONTY'S SPACESHIP IS READY FOR ACTION!

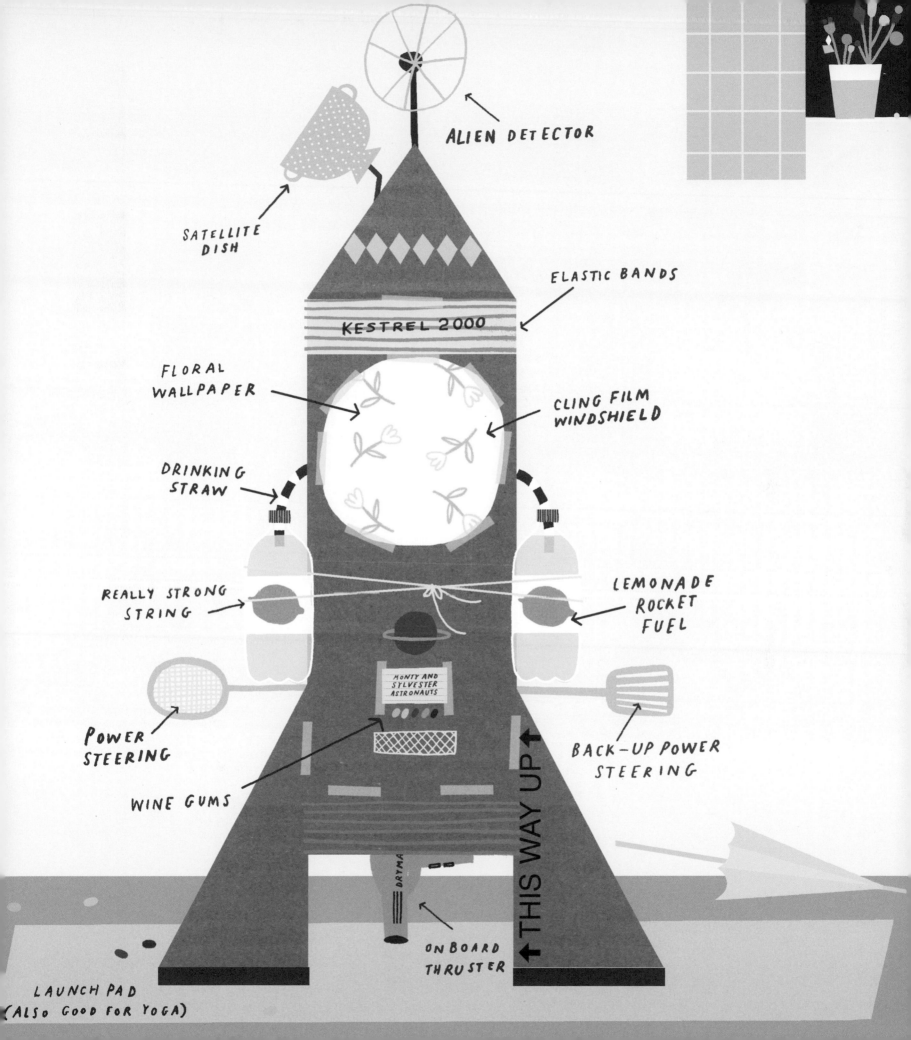

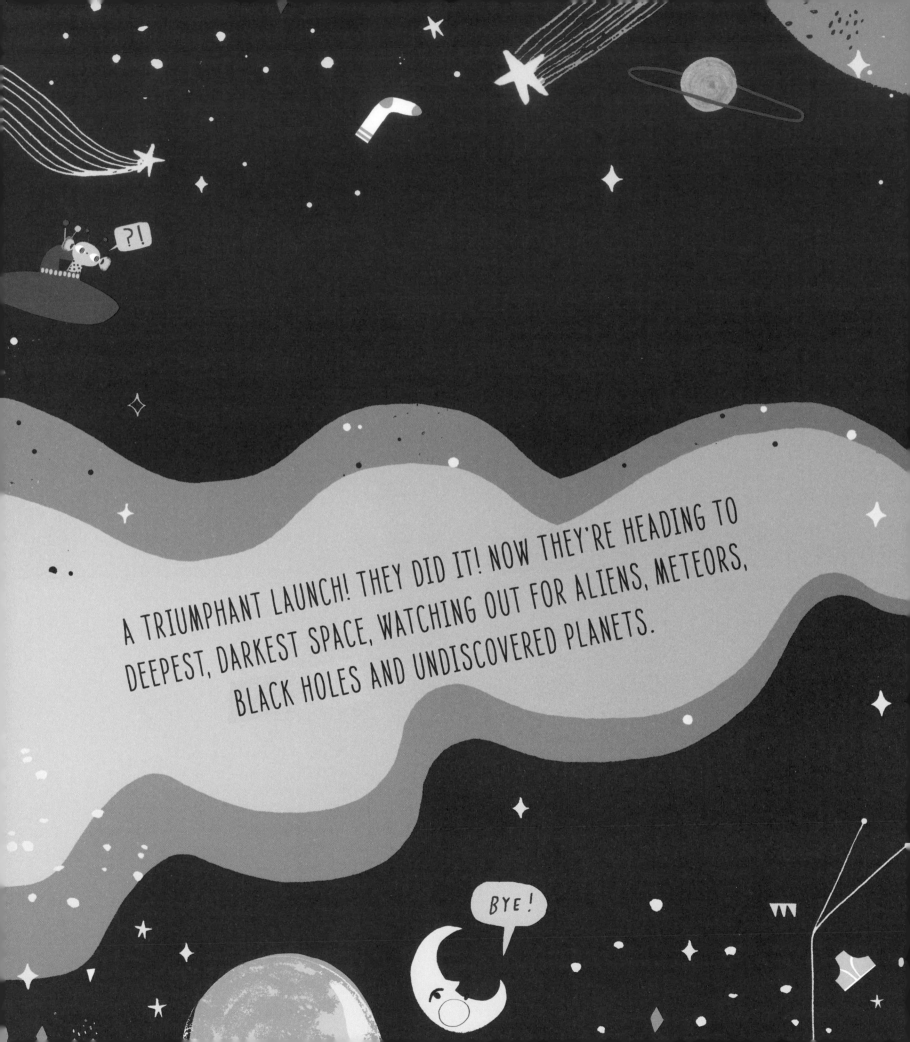

IT'S ALL GOING TO PLAN.

WELL, UNTIL . . . .

# UH-OH.

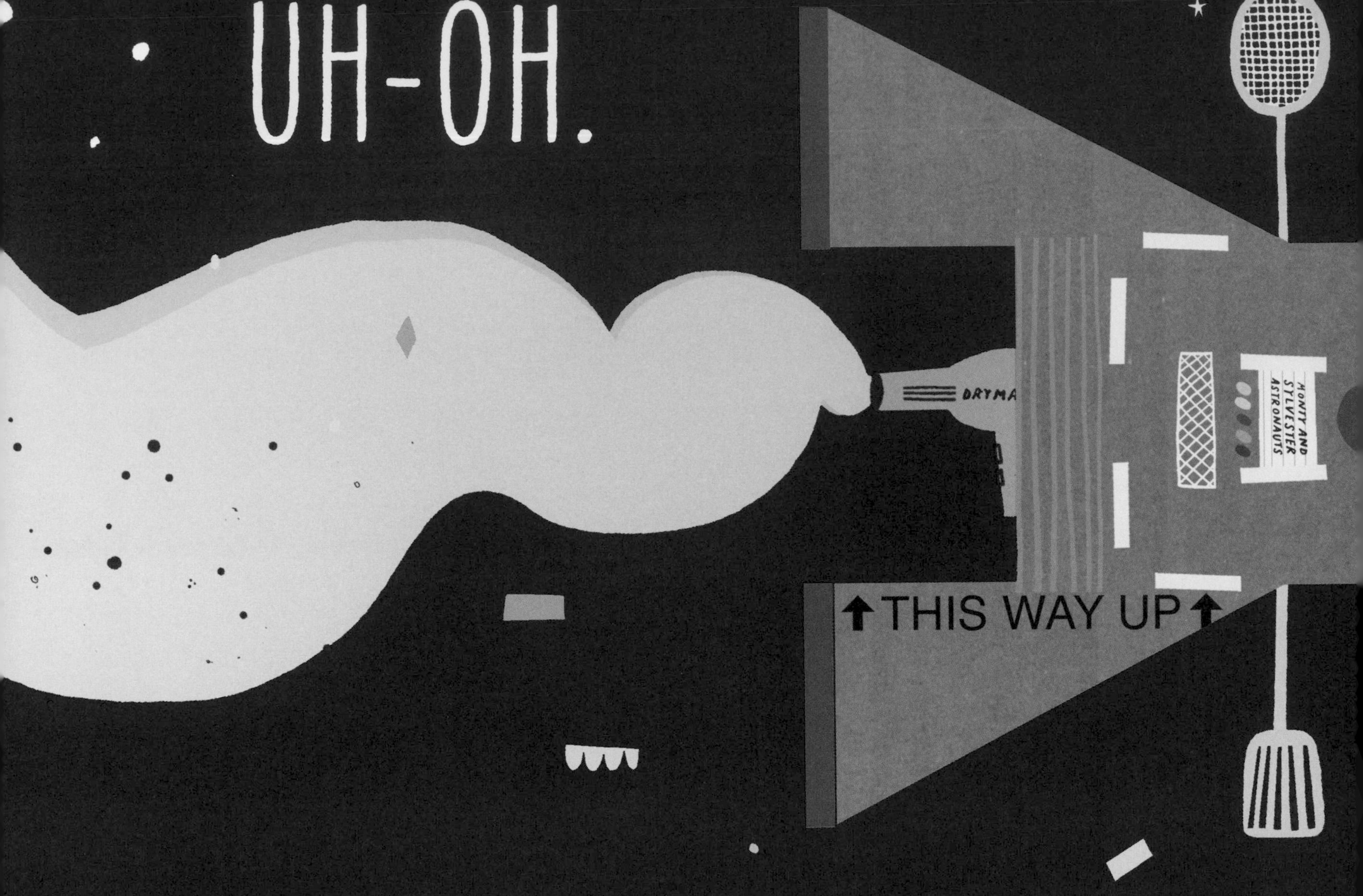


# BLACK HOLE DEAD AHEAD.

UNFORTUNATELY MONTY HAS NO PLAN B!
IS THEIR MISSION OVER ALREADY?

PHEW!

THEY JUST MISSED IT.

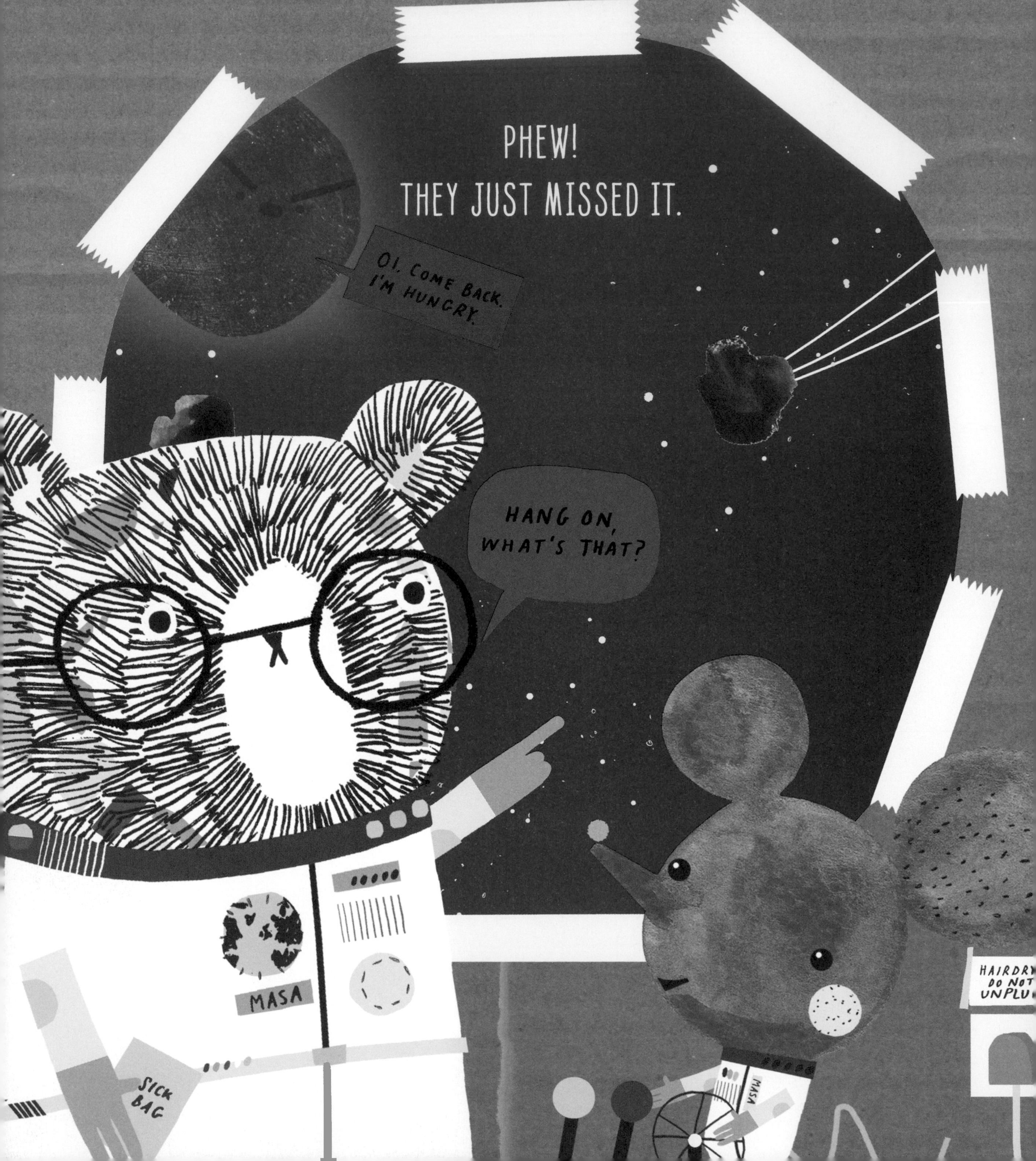

IT'S A GALACTIC-SIZE METEOR SHOWER!
MONTY, WE HAVE A PROBLEM
HELP!
KESTREL 2000
MONTY AND SYLVESTER ASTRONAUTS
DON'T WORRY, SYLVESTER. I'VE ENGAGED THE METEOR SHIELD!
WHIZZ
WHOOSH
DOINK
CRACK
OH

THAT'S THAT THEN,
## MISSION OVER.

IS THIS THE END OF
MONTY AND SYLVESTER?

THERE'S ONLY ONE LITTLE ALIEN HERE. HE WON'T MIND IF MONTY AND SYLVESTER CLAIM THIS PLANET.

OOPS, SPOKE TOO SOON.
THEY'RE IN <u>BIG TROUBLE</u> NOW.

INCREDIBLE, WITHOUT UNDERSTANDING EACH OTHER, THEY HAVE MANAGED TO MAKE FRIENDS! IT SEEMS THE ALIENS THINK MONTY AND SYLVESTER ARE RATHER SPECIAL.

MONTY AND SYLVESTER HAVE BEEN TREATED LIKE ROYALTY.

BUT IT'S TIME TO GET BACK TO PLANET EARTH AND

TELL THEIR FRIENDS ABOUT THEIR ASTRONOMICAL SUCCESS!

HI EVERYONE.
WE'RE BACK FROM
OUTER SPACE!
WE DID IT!

WE FOUND A NEW
PLANET!
PLANET MONTY!

# THE END.
### A TOPNOTCH JOB WELL DONE.
### MISSION COMPLETE!

TIME TO RELAX, READ
THE PAPERS, EAT SOME
MORE CHEESE AND PLAN
TOMORROW'S MISSION.

**SPORT** GOAL **THE NEWS**

DOG EATS BALL

FREE PLANT POT INSIDE **NEW PLANET DISCOVERED**

SOCKS NOW ON SALE

I ♥ EARTH

D.I.Y SUBMARINES